# Henry and Mudge

# HENRY AND MUDGE

## CYNTHIA RYLANT

### ILLUSTRATED BY
### SUÇIE STEVENSON

GOLLANCZ CHILDREN'S PAPERBACKS

LONDON

For Nate and his dog – CR
For Grandma Biffy – SS

# Contents

# Henry

Henry had no brothers
and no sisters.
"I want a brother,"
he told his parents.
"Sorry," they said.
Henry had no friends
in his street.

"I want to live
in a different street,"
he told his parents.
"Sorry," they said.
Henry had no pets
at home.
"I want to have a dog,"
he told his parents.
"Sorry," they *almost* said.

But first they looked

at their house

with no brothers and sisters.

Then they looked

at their street

with no children.

Then they looked

at Henry's face.

Then they looked at each other.

"Okay," they said.

"I want to hug you!"

Henry told his parents.

And he did.

# Mudge

Henry searched for a dog.

"Not just any dog," said Henry.

"Not a short one," he said.

"Not a curly one," he said.

"And no pointed ears."

Then he found Mudge.
Mudge had floppy ears,
not pointed.
And Mudge had straight fur,
not curly.
But Mudge was short.
"Because he's a puppy,"
Henry said.
"He'll grow."

And he did!

He grew out of his puppy basket.

He grew out of his dog basket.

He grew out of seven collars

in a row.

And when he finally

stopped growing . . .

he weighed one hundred and eighty pounds,
he stood three feet tall,
and he drooled.
"I'm glad you're not short,"
Henry said.

And Mudge licked him,
then sat on him.

# Henry

Henry used to walk
to school alone.
When he walked
he used to worry about
tornadoes,
ghosts,
biting dogs,
and bullies.

He walked as fast
as he could.
He looked straight ahead.
He never looked back.
But now he walked to school
with Mudge.

And now when he walked,
he thought about
vanilla ice cream,
rain,
rocks,
and good dreams.
He walked to school,
but not too fast.
He walked to school,
and sometimes backwards.

He walked to school
and patted Mudge's big head,
happy.

# Mudge

Mudge loved Henry's room.

He loved the dirty socks.

He loved the stuffed bear.

He loved the fish tank.

But mostly he loved

Henry's bed.

Because in Henry's bed
was Henry.
Mudge loved to climb in
with Henry.
Then he loved
to smell him.

He smelled his lemon hair.

He smelled his milky mouth.

He smelled his soapy ears.

He smelled his chocolate fingers.

Then he put his head
by Henry's head.
He looked at the fish tank.
He looked at the bear.
He looked at Henry.
He licked him.
And he fell asleep.

# Mudge

One day Mudge took a walk
without Henry.
The sun was shining,
the birds were flying,
the grass smelled sweet.
Mudge couldn't wait for Henry.
So he left.

He went down one road,

sniffing the bushes,

then down another road,

kicking up dust.

He went through a field,

across a stream,

into some pine trees.

And when he came out
on the other side,
he was lost.

He couldn't smell Henry.
He couldn't smell
his front porch.
He couldn't smell
the street he lived in.
Mudge looked all around
and didn't see anything
or anyone
he knew.

He whined a little,
alone without Henry.
Then he lay down,
alone without Henry.
He missed Henry's bed.

Henry

Henry thought Mudge

would be with him always.

He thought Mudge

made everything safe.

He thought Mudge

would never go away.

And when Mudge did go away,
when Henry called and called
but Mudge didn't come,
Henry's heart hurt
and he cried for an hour.
But when he finished crying,
Henry said, "Mudge loves me.
He wouldn't leave.
He must be lost."

So Henry walked and walked,
and he called and called,
and he looked and looked
for his dog Mudge.
He walked down one road,
then down another road.
The sun shone as Henry ran
through a field,
calling and calling.

30

The birds flew past
as he stood beside a stream,
calling and calling.

And the tears fell again
as he looked at the
empty pine trees
for his lost dog.
"*Mudge!*" he called, one last time.

And Mudge woke up
from his lonely sleep,
then
came
running.

# Henry and Mudge

Every day when Henry woke up,

he saw Mudge's big head.

And every day

when Mudge woke up,

he saw Henry's small face.

They ate breakfast
at the same time;

they ate supper
at the same time.

And when Henry was at school,
Mudge just lay around
and waited.
Mudge never went for a walk
without Henry again.
And Henry never worried
that Mudge would leave.

Because sometimes, in their dreams,
they saw long silent roads,
big wide fields,
deep streams,
and pine trees.

In those dreams,
Mudge was alone
and Henry was alone.
So when Mudge woke up
and knew Henry was with him,
he remembered the dream
and stayed closer.

And when Henry woke up
and knew Mudge was with him,
he remembered the dream
and the looking
and the calling
and the fear
and he knew
he would never lose Mudge
again.